THE BOY WHO LIVED

WITH THE BEARS

AND OTHER IROQUOIS STORIES

THE BOY WHO LIVED WITH THE BEARS

. . . .

AND OTHER IROQUOIS STORIES

Told by JOSEPH BRUCHAC
Illustrated by MURV JACOB

PARABOLA BOOKS
NEW YORK

JACOB
2004

My grateful thanks to my daughter, Jana,
for her assistance with designing and painting this book.

—M.J.

This title is derived from an audio series of Native American tales documenting representative
tribal cultures in the United States and Canada. The PARABOLA Storytime Series®
has been developed and produced by PARABOLA MAGAZINE in collaboration with leading
Native American artists, storytellers, and musicians.

The Boy Who Lived with the Bears
and Other Iroquois Stories
Text copyright © 1995 by Joseph Bruchac • Illustrations copyright © 1995 by Murv Jacob
Hardcover edition originally published by HarperCollins Publishers.

Library of Congress Cataloging-in-Publication Data
Bruchac, Joseph, 1942–
The boy who lived with the bears : and other Iroquois stories / told by Joseph Bruchac ; illustrated by Murv Jacob.
p. cm. -- (The Parabola storytime series)
Originally published: New York : HarperCollins, c1995.
Summary: Presents a collection of traditional Iroquois stories in which animals learn about the importance of caring
and responsibility and the dangers of selfishness and pride.
ISBN 0–930407–61–X (pbk. : alk. paper)
1. Iroquois Indians—Folklore. 2. Legends—New York (State) [1. Iroquois Indians—Folklore. 2. Indians of North
America—Folklore. 3. Animals—Folklore. 4. Folklore—North America.] I. Jacob, Murv, ill. II. Title. III. Series

E99.I7.B83 2003
398.2'089'9755—dc22

2003058106

Typography by Tom Starace
1   2   3   4   5   6   7   8   9   10
❖
First Paperback Edition 2003

To the children and the teachers
of the Onondaga Indian School with thanks for all they have taught me
—J.B.

This book is respectfully
dedicated to our dear friends Robert and Evelyn Conley.
—M.J.

CONTENTS

Introduction   9

Rabbit and Fox   15

The Boy Who Lived With the Bears   22

How the Birds Got Their Feathers   34

Turtle Makes War on Man   40

Chipmunk and Bear   53

Rabbit's Snow Dance   57

INTRODUCTION

It is the time when the snows are deep and the wind's voice circles the big Bear Clan longhouse. It is Tsiotorkowa, the Coldest Moon, when the nights are the longest. People are gathered round the most central of the five fires. Those fires serve as communal hearths for the twenty families who live here, all members of the Bear Clan, for each longhouse is headed by a clan mother. And just as the father's name is inherited among present-day Americans, the children all inherit the clan of their mother.

But this evening it is not only the Bear Clan women, the husbands who have come to live with the families of their wives, the elders, and the many children who are here. This evening people have come crowding in from the other four longhouses that are also part of this village surrounded by cornfields. Almost all the people of the clans of the Turtle, the Wolf, the Snipe, and the Eel have come as guests, from the oldest to those so small their mothers must carry them. They are here because of the man in his

late middle years who sits now by the fire, looking around the circle of expectant faces. His name is Crosses Many Rivers and he is from another village a six days' walk west from here along the Mohawk River. He was a great hunter and warrior in his youth, and his name went out among his people. Now wherever he travels, his name precedes him and every longhouse opens its door to him, for he is a storyteller.

Crosses Many Rivers clears his throat, and what little noise the people are making suddenly subsides. There is only the sound of the crackling fire, the wind, and hushed breathing. He puts down the clay pipe that he has just been given on his arrival—the kind of special gift that is often given to welcome the storyteller. He reaches into the deerskin bag that hangs at his waist, and from it pulls a bear claw. "Now," he says, "hear a story. Hear the story of the boy who became a bear. Hoh!"

And as one, the people answer back, "Henh!"

As a storyteller, I often imagine myself in that sort of old-time setting when I begin a tale. It is not hard for me to do, for I live in the part of North America that was cared for by the Iroquois for thousands of years. For more than thirty years I have listened to Iroquois elders tell these stories—though the stories might be told more often today in a living room while the television is still playing or over a loudspeaker at a powwow or an Indian festival open to the general public than around a campfire or inside a long-house shingled with the bark of the elm tree. I live, too, in the house where I was raised

INTRODUCTION

by my maternal grandfather, a gentle man whose Native ancestry was Abenaki, an Algonquin nation with a long history of living next to and among the People of the Longhouse.

When my own children came into this world—more than two decades ago now—I began telling them these stories. Before long, I found myself telling the stories to other children and to adults, and I began traveling as those old storytellers did long ago. I crossed many rivers and found myself as welcomed as they were. The gifts that I've received have been as special to me as those given the old storytellers. One of those gifts, given me by Dewasentah, the Clan Mother of the Eel Clan at the Onondaga Nation, is an Iroquois name—Gah Neh Goh He Yoh, which means "The Good Mind." It is an acknowledgment of the power of the words that a good storyteller has been given, and a reminder of the responsibility involved in being one who carries those words.

The Iroquois call themselves Haudenosaunee. It means "People of the Longhouse" and is a reminder of the type of dwelling they lived in before the Europeans came. Each longhouse might be as much as thirty feet wide and eighty feet long and would hold a number of families, all linked together by a common clan descent. There were five original Iroquois nations, and they viewed their alliance, which was called The Great League of Peace, as being in the shape of a longhouse. The Mohawk People to the east along the Mohawk and Hudson rivers are called The Keepers of the Eastern

Door. The present-day city of Albany is on Mohawk land. The Seneca to the far west, near the great falls of Niagara, are The Keepers of the Western Door. The Onondaga are The Keepers of the Central Fire and the symbolic Great Tree of Peace, whose branches are meant to shelter any who wish to join the alliance. Syracuse is on Onondaga land. To the east of them are the Oneida People, and to the southwest, among the Finger Lakes, the Cayuga Nation.

The Iroquois today, who number more than 20,000 in New York State alone, remain proud of their heritage and aware of their language and traditions. Like their ancestors, they are concerned about finding ways to create peace and harmony in a world where war remains a danger. Iroquois elders such as Oren Lyons travel all over the world speaking about ecological issues and trying to help people see that our earth is alive and must be treated well so that our children's children can survive. Like the Longhouse People of old, the present-day Iroquois worry about the children of the world and want to see them taught well and treated with respect.

Today, after many years of being misunderstood and described as warlike savages, the People of the Longhouse are finally being viewed with respect. Their large-scale agriculture, using the Three Sisters (corn, beans, and squash), is now being recognized as one of the most sophisticated and efficient farming systems ever devised. Their Great League of Peace is now seen by many historians as a direct influence on the framing of the United States Constitution. The balanced roles of women (who headed

INTRODUCTION

the families and chose the leaders of the people) and men are an example for the modern world. The approval that I have received in the past from Iroquois elders for my telling of these stories—which teach important lessons about caring and responsibility and the dangers of selfishness and pride—is one of the greatest of honors I have received. Because of that approval and because these stories still have so much to offer, I continue to tell these tales each winter. And now I share them in this book.

RABBIT AND FOX

Long ago, back when the animals could talk and the people could understand them, Rabbit was out walking around. It was a beautiful winter day. The snow was on the ground, and as Rabbit walked he made tracks in the snow. Nothing seemed to be wrong with the world until suddenly, from behind a bush, out jumped Fox.

"Urr," said Fox. "I am Fox. I am going to catch you. I am going to eat you!" Rabbit quickly began to run. He ran as fast as he could, leaving Fox far behind. But Fox, seeing Rabbit's tracks in the snow, began to follow them.

Now, far ahead, Rabbit slipped off his moccasins. He blew on them and said, "Go ahead, make tracks!" The moccasins began to make tracks in the snow, and Rabbit hid behind a bush.

Soon Fox came along following those moccasin tracks, and as soon as he passed by Rabbit, Rabbit quickly ran away in the opposite direction. Before too long, though, Fox caught up with the moccasins. He saw he had been fooled. "Huhh," said Fox. "I am going to catch that Rabbit. I am going to eat that Rabbit!"

Fox turned around and backtracked and found the place where Rabbit had slipped away through the bushes. He followed Rabbit's tracks through the snow until he came to a clearing in the forest, and there in that clearing Rabbit's tracks went around and around and ended right where an old woman was sitting.

This old woman had a blanket wrapped around her shoulders, and she had on a very strange hat—it had two feathers sticking up from the top of it. Fox came right up to that old woman. "Old woman," he said, "have you seen a rabbit go by here?"

The old woman looked at Fox, and she wiggled her nose in a funny way, and she said, "Why, yes, I did see a rabbit go by here. He was a very skinny rabbit indeed. There was no meat on his bones. No one would want to eat that rabbit."

· ·

But Fox, he said, "Huhh, I am Fox. I am going to catch that rabbit and I am going to eat that rabbit!"

"Uh-huh," said the old woman, looking at Fox. "I can see you are a great hunter. You will surely catch that poor rabbit. You are obviously one of the greatest hunters of all. Perhaps you are almost as great a hunter as my son. My son hunts for only one thing, though."

"What is that?" said Fox.

"He hunts only for foxes," said the old woman. "In fact, there he is now, right behind you."

Fox turned around to look. There was no one there, but as he turned to look, that old woman threw off her blanket, grabbed a club, leaped high in the air, and *Whonk!* hit Fox right on top of the head. Then she ran away, because it was not an old woman at all— it was Rabbit.

Now, when Fox woke up he had a big bump on top of his head. "Huhh," he said. "That was Rabbit, and I am going to catch that rabbit. I am going to eat that rabbit!" And he began following Rabbit's tracks there in the snow.

He followed those tracks for a long time, until he came to a grove of trees. And there, sitting at the edge of that grove of trees, was an old medicine man. The old medicine man had a blanket wrapped around him. He had a pot of soup cooking in front of him, and this old medicine man had on a very strange cap with two feathers sticking out of the top of it. And the rabbit's tracks ended right there, where that old medicine man was sitting.

Fox came right up to him. "Old man," Fox said, "have you seen a rabbit go by here?"

"Uh-huh," said the old man, "indeed I did see a rabbit go by here. It was a rabbit who looked to be very sick. In fact, if anyone were to eat that rabbit, he would become sick too."

"Huhh," said Fox. "I am Fox. I am going to catch that rabbit and I am going to eat that rabbit!"

"Ahh," said the old medicine man. "I can see you will do as you say. You are very strong and determined. I can see this now. But tell me, my son, how did you get that bump on top of your head?"

"Huhh," said Fox. "I, uh, I ran into a tree last night."

"Uh-huh," said the old medicine man. "Come and sit down in front of me, my son. Let me doctor your bump."

So Fox sat down with his back to the old medicine man. The old medicine man began to rub the top of Fox's head. Suddenly the old medicine man shouted, "Look! Over there on the other side of the clearing, the eagle is flying down!"

And when Fox looked to see the eagle, the old medicine man threw off his blanket, picked up a club, leaped high in the air, and *Whomp!* hit Fox right on top of the head. And then he ran away, for it was no medicine man at all—it was Rabbit.

When Fox woke up again, he had a bump on top of the bump on top of his head. "Huhh," Fox said. "Now I see what has happened. I am going to catch that rabbit. I am going to eat that rabbit, and if I find anyone or anything with two feathers, I will know they are Rabbit and I will eat them." And Fox began to run, following Rabbit's tracks in the snow.

Up ahead of Fox, Rabbit was getting tired. "Oh," Rabbit said to himself, "I thought that Fox would give up by now. I can't think of

any more tricks. What can I do?" Then Rabbit saw an old rotten log by the side of the trail, and that old rotten log had two sticks coming out of it that looked a little bit like feathers. Rabbit ran toward that log and leaped as high as he could, landing in the bushes on the other side. And he held his breath and waited.

Along came Fox following the tracks, and he saw the tracks ended right by that log. "Huhh," said Fox. "Here is where the tracks end. Where is Rabbit? There is only this log. Ahh, but this log has two feathers. This is no log at all. This is Rabbit!"

Fox sniffed that log. "Huhh," he said. "It even smells like a rotten log. But it must be Rabbit." Fox took a bite of that rotten log. "Ugh, this tastes terrible. It even tastes like a rotten log. But I know it must be Rabbit. Rabbit, I am Fox. I have caught you, and now I am going to eat you!" And with that, Fox began to eat that rotten log. Bite after bite, he ate that log, until he had eaten the entire thing. He did not feel well at all. He looked at his stomach, which was sticking out like a bowl. "Uhhh," said Fox. "Maybe

I don't like to eat Rabbits after all." And he went home feeling very sick.

Rabbit came out from behind the bushes and did a little dance there in the snow, singing, "Fox, you didn't catch this Rabbit! Fox, you didn't eat this Rabbit!" And then Rabbit ran away.

That is how that story goes. *Ho? Hey.*

THE BOY WHO LIVED WITH THE BEARS

Long ago, in a small village of the Haudenosaunee people, there lived a little boy whose parents had died. This boy was living with his uncle, as was the custom in those days, for it was said that no child would ever be without parents.

But this boy's uncle did not have a straight mind. Although it was his duty to take care of his nephew, he resented the fact that he had this boy to care for. Instead of taking care of him, he treated him badly. He dressed him in ragged clothes; he gave him only

scraps of food to eat; he never even called the boy by his name. He just would say, "Hey, you, get out of my way!"

Now, this boy had always been taught by his parents to treat elders with respect. So he tried to do everything he could to please his uncle. His uncle was very respected in the village because he was a great hunter. When he and his dog went out, they always brought back game. One day, the uncle woke up with an idea in his mind. It was a twisted-mind idea, for what the uncle thought was this: "Too long have I been bothered with this troublesome boy. Today, I will get rid of him."

And so he called, "You, come here!" The boy quickly came, because he wanted to please his uncle. The uncle said, "You and I, we're going to go hunting together."

They left the lodge and started for the woods, and that was when the boy noticed something strange. He said, "Uncle, aren't you going to take your dog?" The uncle looked at the boy and said, "Today, you will be my dog."

Then the boy noticed another thing that was strange—they were

going toward the north. In the village, when people went hunting, they would go to the east, or the south, or the west, but they would never go to the north, because there, it was said, strange things happened in the forest. Farther and farther the boy and his uncle went, away from any of the trails that people would follow, farther and farther to the north. The boy stayed close behind his uncle.

Finally, they came to a small clearing in the deep forest. On the other side, in the hillside, there was a small cave. The uncle said, "There are animals in there. You are my dog. Crawl in and chase them out." The boy was frightened, but then he thought back to what his parents had always told him: "Do what your elders say. Trust your elders."

So he crawled into the cave, but there was nothing there, no animal at all. As he turned around and began to crawl out, the circle of light that was the mouth of the cave suddenly vanished—the cave mouth had been blocked by a big stone. That was when the boy realized that his uncle meant to leave him there, and he began to cry.

But as his tears came, he remembered the song his mother had

taught him to sing when he needed a friend. Softly, he began to sing:

"Weyanna, weyanna, weyanna, hey.
Weyanna, weyanna, weyanna, hey.
Weyanna, weyanna, weyanna, hey.
Wey, hey yo-o-o, wey hey yo."

Then he stopped, because it seemed as if he could hear soft singing answering him on the other side of that rock. So he sang a little louder:

"Weyanna, weyanna, weyanna, hey.
Weyanna, weyanna, weyanna, hey.
Weyanna, weyanna, weyanna, hey.
Wey, hey yo-o-o, wey hey yo."

And from the other side of that rock came back:

"Wey, hey yo-o-o, wey hey yo."

The boy knew now that someone was out there, singing back to him, so he sang louder again. From the other side of the rock the song came back, strongly now. Then, together, the song was sung from both sides of the stone, and it ended together very loudly:

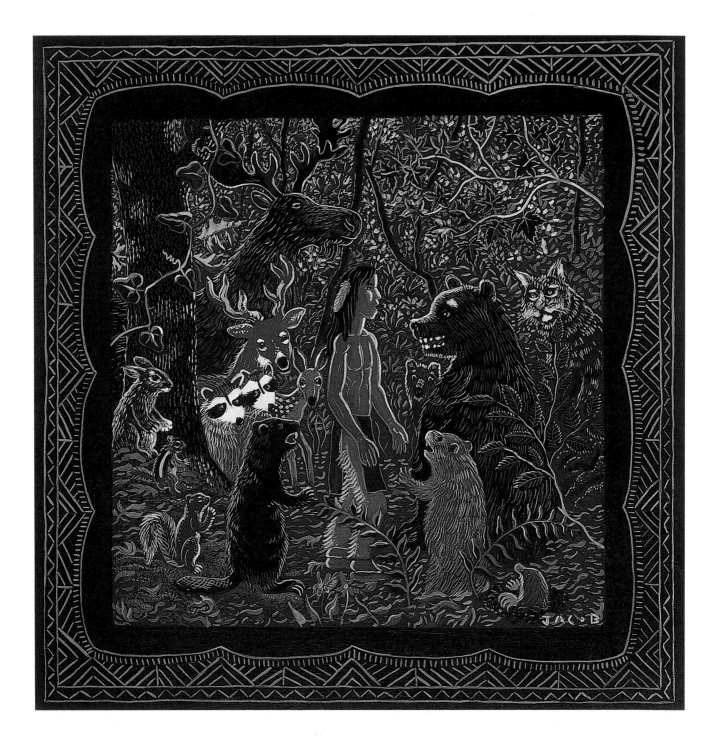

"Wey, hey yo-o-o, wey hey yo."

As the song ended, the rock was rolled away, and the boy crawled out into the bright sunlight, blinking his eyes. All around him in the clearing many people were gathered: big people, small people, tall people, skinny people, fat people, people of all shapes and sizes. He blinked his eyes again, and he saw they were not people at all. They were animals, all the animals of the forest: bears, deer, foxes, wolves, beavers, muskrats, and even the small animals—squirrels, woodchucks, chipmunks, moles. All of them were gathered there and all were looking straight at him. He stood up, and all of those animals took one step toward him! The boy did not know what would happen next. And that was when an old grandmother woodchuck shuffled up to him, poked him in the leg, and said, "Grandson, we heard your song. Do you need a friend?"

"Yes," said the boy. "I do need a friend. You've come to help me?"

"Yes," said the old grandmother woodchuck, "but where is your family? Why are you here, trapped in this cave?" The boy shook his

head sadly. "My parents died, and only my uncle was left to care for me. But he did not want me. He put me in this cave and left me here to die, so I have no family anywhere in the world."

The old grandmother woodchuck said, "Grandson, we will be your family! Pick any of us, and we will adopt you!" The boy looked around. All the animals were looking at him, but how could he decide?

"My friends," he said, "tell me what your lives are like. Then I can decide which one I will come and live with."

So the animals began to tell him about their lives: The mole told him how he lived in a warm burrow and dug in the earth and ate delicious worms; the beaver described how he swam underwater and lived in a warm lodge and ate tree bark. The boy thanked each animal politely, but said that he did not have the claws to dig like the mole, and that he could not hold his breath and swim underwater like the beaver.

Then the old mother bear came up. "My boy, you would like to be a bear. We take our time going through the forest. We eat the

most delicious honey and berries. We sleep in our warm cave. And my two children here will play with you as much as you want." The boy quickly said, "I will be a bear."

And indeed, it was as the old mother bear said. Their lives were very good together. They took their time going through the forest. They ate delicious berries and honey, and the boy grew fat and happy. The bear cubs would wrestle and play with him as much as he wanted. In fact, he began to look like a bear himself, because when they wrestled and played, if their claws scratched him, hair would grow there, so that after some time had passed, that boy looked just like a bear, covered with black hair himself.

For two seasons, they lived this way. But then one day, as they were walking through the forest, the old mother bear stopped suddenly and said, "Listen! . . . Listen!"

Well, the boy listened. And before long, he heard the sound of feet walking through the forest, stepping on twigs and brushing past the leaves. The old mother bear began to laugh. "That is the sound of a hunter trying to hunt the bear. But he makes so much

noise going through the forest, we call him Heavy Foot. He will never catch a bear!" And so they continued on their way.

Another day came, and again as they walked through the forest, the old mother bear stopped and said, "Listen!" The boy could hear the sound of someone talking to himself, saying, "Ahhh, it is a very good day for hunting. Ah-ha, today I will surely catch a bear! Uh, yes, uh, I will probably catch more than one bear, for I am a great hunter!"

Old mother bear began to laugh. "That's the one who talks to himself while he hunts. We call him Flapping Jaws. He will never catch a bear!"

And so it went on. Each day they listened. They heard the hunter called Bumps into Trees, and the one called Falls in the Lake. None of these hunters was good enough to catch a bear.

But then one day, as they walked along, the old mother bear said, "Stop. Listen!" For a long time, the boy could hear nothing. Then, very, very faintly, he could hear the sound of soft feet, moving through the forest. But it did not sound like two feet. It did

not sound like four feet. It sounded like two feet and four feet.

The old mother bear quickly nodded. She said, "This is the one we fear. It is Two Legs and Four Legs. We must RUN!" And she began to run. The boy and the two cubs ran behind her through the forest, but Two Legs and Four Legs were behind them. They ran through the swamps, but Two Legs and Four Legs were getting closer. They ran up the hills, but still Two Legs and Four Legs followed, and now the boy could hear behind them a sound growing louder: *"Wuf, wuf, wuf, wuf, wuf!"* And the boy knew that Two Legs and Four Legs were very close behind.

They came to a clearing where an old tree had fallen. It was hollow. The boy and the two cubs and the old mother bear went into that hollow log to hide.

The boy listened. He heard Two Legs and Four Legs come into the clearing and right up to the log. And then everything became quiet.

"Perhaps they've gone away," the boy thought. But then he began to smell smoke. Smoke was coming into the log! Two Legs had

made a fire and was blowing the smoke into the log to make them come out.

It was just at that moment that the boy remembered that he, too, was a Two Legs. He was a person, a human being, and that was a hunter and a dog out there. The boy shouted, "Stop! Don't hurt my family!" And upon these words, the smoke stopped coming into the log.

The boy crawled out, blinking his eyes against the light. There in front of him stood the hunter, and the hunter was his uncle! The uncle stared at the boy. The boy stood up and came closer. The uncle reached out and touched him, and all the hair fell off the boy's body, and he looked like a person again.

"My nephew!" said the uncle. "Is it truly you? Are you alive?"

"Yes, I am, Uncle," said the boy.

"How could this be?" said the uncle. "I went back to the cave, because I realized I had done a twisted-mind thing. But when I got there, the stone had been rolled away. There were the tracks of many animals. I thought they had eaten you."

"No," said the boy. "The bears adopted me. They are my family now, Uncle. You must treat them well."

The uncle nodded. He said, "My nephew, your words are true. Call your family out. I will greet them and I will be their friend." So the boy called, and the old mother bear and the two cubs came out from the log; they came out and sniffed the hunter. He stood there patiently, letting them approach him.

From that day on, the hunter and his nephew were a family, and the bears were part of their family. And ever since then, this story has been told to remind parents and elders always to treat their children well and to show as much love in their hearts as a bear holds in its heart for its children.

That is how the story goes. *Ho? Hey.*

How the Birds Got Their Feathers

Long ago, back when the world was new, the birds had no feathers. It was difficult for them in those days. When the sun shone down brightly, they were too hot. When the wind blew and the seasons turned to the long white time, they were cold and they shivered in the forest. And so it was that the Creator took pity on them and sent down a message to them in a dream.

All the birds gathered together in council to discuss the dream they had all had, the dream they knew was a message from the Creator. The message was this: If they would appoint one bird to be

their messenger, that bird could go to the Skyland and bring back clothing for all the birds. The Eagle, who was the chief, sat on the council rock and began the discussion: Who could fly that long distance, high into the Skyland, to bring back clothing for the birds?

Everyone wanted to go, but some of the birds were too small; their wings were too weak. The great Eagle could fly the highest of all, but as the chief of the birds he had to stay with his people. Finally it was decided that Buzzard, with his long, strong wings, would be the one to fly to the Skyland with the message that they were ready to accept the Creator's gift of clothing.

Buzzard began to fly. He flew and he flew through the sky. He flew for so long that he became hungry; he had forgotten to eat before he left on his journey. He looked down, and there by the side of the lake he saw some rotten fish. He was so hungry that he flew down and he ate those rotten fish. Then, feeling better, he began to fly again.

Buzzard flew higher and higher, up toward the Skyland. Higher and higher he went, so high that the heat of the sun shone down

and burned the top of his bald head. But he was determined to carry the message of all the birds up to the Creator, and so he continued.

Up and up he flew, until at last he came to the Skyland, where the Creator waited. "Buzzard," the Creator said, "you have done well. You have been brave and determined. You have carried the message of your people to me. I see that you wish to receive this gift of clothing from me. All the birds will have clothes, which you will take back to them. Buzzard, since you were the messenger, and you were so determined and brave, I will give you the first choice of clothing to wear."

The Creator took Buzzard to a place where many suits of clothing hung, all of them made of beautiful feathers. Buzzard looked around. As the messenger for all the birds, he would have to pick the very best suit of all. As he looked, the Creator came to him and said, "Now, Buzzard, you must remember this. Any one of these suits of feathers will fit you when you put it on. If you do not like it, simply take it off, and it will go to another bird. But remember,

once you have tried it on and taken it off, it can never be yours again." Buzzard understood, and he began to look.

Now, there was a beautiful suit with red feathers and a little black mask. Buzzard tried it on. It was very bright and nice, he thought, but only red? That was not enough, so he took that suit off and it went to Cardinal.

There was another suit with black on it, a little bit of white, a gray back, and a red vest. Buzzard tried that on. Hmmm, he thought, not quite showy enough. That one went to Robin.

There was a yellow-and-black suit. This too was nice, but the messenger of all the birds must have many colors in his suit of feathers, thought Buzzard. So he took that suit off too; it went to Goldfinch.

Buzzard tried on one suit of feathers after another. The Creator patiently waited and watched, until finally, Buzzard tried on a suit that fit so tightly, it didn't cover his legs. It left his bald, red, sunburned head bare, and the feathers were brown and dirty. Buzzard looked at himself, and Buzzard was not pleased. "Ugh!" he said.

"This suit is the worst of them all!" And the Creator said, "Buzzard, it is the last of all the suits. It has to be yours."

So it came to be that from that day on, Buzzard wore that suit of dirty feathers. And ever since then, too, because he stopped to eat those rotten fish on his journey, Buzzard has had an appetite for things that are long dead. But still, when he flies high in the sky with his wings spread, up there close to the Skyland, you may remember that he was the messenger for all the birds. Despite his dirty suit of feathers, he still has reason to be proud.

And that is how that story goes. *Ho? Hey.*

Turtle Makes War on Man

Long ago, back in the days when the animals could talk and the people could understand them, Turtle woke up one morning with a great idea. "Too long," Turtle said, "too long have human beings hunted the animals. It is time that we, the animals, joined together, and made war on human beings and wiped them out."

So Turtle got some red paint and painted his cheeks to show that he was serious about taking the path to war. He went down to the

river, and he got out his small canoe. He climbed in, and he began to paddle down the river, and as he went, he sang his canoe song. He sang:

> *"Kai oh wah gee nay yo, oh hey ho hey,*
> *Kai oh wah gee nay, kai oh wah gee nay.*
> *Kai oh wah gee nay yo, hey hey ho ho,*
> *Kai oh wah gee nay, kai oh wah gee nay."*

And as he paddled down the river, there on the bank he saw a big animal standing on its hind legs. It waved at Turtle. It growled and said, "Turtle, take me with you. I want to go and make war on the human beings."

It was Bear, the biggest of all the animals. Bear's foot was twice as big as Turtle's canoe. So Turtle thought fast. He said, "You are too slow to go to war with me. If I went to strike the enemy, you would fall behind and you would be no good at all. Only the mightiest warriors can go with Turtle when he makes war. You must stay here." And quickly, Turtle began to paddle his canoe down the river, singing his song:

"Kai oh wah gee nay yo, oh hey ho hey,
Kai oh wah gee nay, kai oh wah gee nay."

Soon the river made a bend, and there, where the river bent, stood another animal. Now, this animal was not as big as Bear. He was standing on all four legs. He had a bushy tail, sharp ears that stood up, and long, sharp teeth. It was Wolf. And Wolf growled at Turtle, and he said, "Turtle, take me with you. I will go and fight the human beings, and I am a fast runner. I am not slow like Bear."

"Well." Turtle looked up at Wolf. Wolf's mouth was big enough to eat Turtle with one bite. Turtle thought fast, and he said, "You are too fast a runner. If you became afraid, you would run away from the battle and I could not catch you to make you fight. Only the mightiest warriors can go with Turtle. You must remain here." Quickly Turtle began to paddle his canoe and sing his song:

"Kai oh wah gee nay yo, oh hey ho hey,
Kai oh wah gee nay, kai oh wah gee nay."

Where the river again made a bend, there stood a third animal. Now this animal was the same size as Turtle. This animal had a

beautiful black coat with a lovely white stripe down the back. When Turtle pulled his canoe in close to the bank, the animal said, "Turtle, take me with you. I will go and fight the human beings."

Turtle looked at this strange animal. "Perhaps you can come with me," he said, "but only the mightiest warriors can come with Turtle. Do you have any weapons?"

This animal said, "Yes, I have one secret weapon."

"There can be no secrets between two mighty warriors such as you and me," said Turtle. "You must show me your secret weapon."

"First I must turn around to do so," the animal said, and he turned around and *Whoosh!* showed Turtle his secret weapon. That weapon was powerful indeed. It knocked Turtle right out of his canoe!

When he had climbed back into his canoe again, he said to this animal, whose name was Skunk, "Your weapon is mighty indeed. You may come with me, but do not use your weapon until we strike the human beings."

Now there were two warriors going down the river together singing:

"Kai oh wah gee nay yo, oh hey ho hey,
Kai oh wah gee nay, kai oh wah gee nay."

Now, on the bank where the river again curved stood the strangest animal of all. This animal had no arms and no legs and looked like a rope all coiled up. As Turtle and Skunk came close, this animal said, "SSSStop. Take me with you. I want to sssstrike the human beings!" It was Rattlesnake.

Turtle looked at Rattlesnake and saw that he would fit into the canoe, but he said, "We are two mighty warriors. We are going to wipe out all the human beings, but only a great warrior can come with us. Do you have any weapons?"

"Yessss, I have one sssssecret weapon," Rattlesnake said.

Turtle shook his head and said, "Do not show it to me. Just get into the canoe." So Rattlesnake crawled into the canoe, and now there were three mighty warriors going down the river singing:

"Kai oh wah gee nay sssyo,
oh hey ho sss,
Kai oh wah gee nay sss
kai oh wah gee nay."

The river began to widen. Where it was its widest, there was a big village of Haudenosaunee people. In this village there were many lodges, and by the riverbank there were many young men standing, practicing games of war. Some were shooting bows and arrows, and some were throwing spears. Some were wrestling with each other. Turtle, seeing this, stopped his canoe in the middle of the river.

The other two warriors waited for the signal to attack, but Turtle said, "Uh, I can see that if these people see us coming, they will be so frightened, they will run away before we can get out of our canoe and wipe them out. We must have a surprise attack." So it was agreed.

They took the canoe very, very softly and quietly over to the bank. They found a little stream that flowed out of the big river,

and they followed that little stream until they came to some bushes. They hid Turtle's canoe, climbed out, and snuck close to the edge of the village. There they made their plans: They would hide themselves all through the night and attack at dawn.

Skunk was the first one to find a place to hide. There was a little spring where the women came to dip water for cooking, and Skunk crawled in among the thick bushes and hid by the edge of the spring.

Rattlesnake was next. He crawled over by one of the lodges where there were some sticks laid out, and he stretched out straight and looked like a stick.

Turtle looked for a place where he could hide. There in front of a lodge were a number of cooking pots turned over and left for the night. Turtle crawled in among the cooking pots, pulled in his head, pulled in his legs and his tail, and looked like a muddy old cooking pot. Then the three great warriors waited for dawn.

When the sun rose in the morning, a woman came from her lodge. She went down to the spring to get some water for cooking.

As she bent over to get her water, Skunk leaped out and *Ahh!* fired his secret weapon. But this woman was very tough and brave. Even though she was coughing and choking, she grabbed Skunk by the neck and began to beat him on top of the head with her fist. She hit him so many times that his head was flattened out. When he woke up, he crawled off into the bushes. To this day, Skunk has a flat head, and he doesn't like to come out during the daytime. He's afraid he might meet that tough woman again.

Now there were only two mighty warriors left, and it was Rattlesnake's turn. Another woman came from her lodge to get some sticks to make her morning fire, but this woman, who had very sharp eyes, saw that something was strange. One of those sticks was twitching its tail. So she backed off and began to pick up some stones, and when she had enough of them, she began to throw them at Rattlesnake. Her aim was so good, she hit him right on the head and flattened his head out. He crawled away as fast as he could. To this day, Rattlesnake has a flat head, and if a Rattlesnake sees you, he won't stretch out like a stick; instead he will coil up and

shake his tail to say, I'm not a stick, I'm not a stick, I'm not a stick.

Now only one mighty warrior was left—Turtle. Inside another lodge there was a man who was lazy. This man had slept late, and his wife poked him and said, "You! Get up! All the other men in the village are out doing things and you are still asleep. The least you can do for me is to go out and bring in the cooking pot."

So this man, yawning, stretching, blinking his eyes, walked outside to the cooking pots and bent over to pick up the first one he saw, even though it was very old and dirty-looking. But it wasn't a cooking pot. It was Turtle, and as soon as the man picked him up, Turtle shot his head out and grabbed the man, right by the leg.

"Ow!" shouted the man. "Let go!" But Turtle does not let go until he is ready. "Let go!" the man shouted, but Turtle just bit harder. The man pulled out a stick and began to hit Turtle on his back many times, so many times that it cracked Turtle's shell, but Turtle did not let go.

"AHH!" said the man. "I am going to drag you over and put you into that big fire there!"

That frightened Turtle. Turtle does not like fire. So Turtle thought fast, and without opening his mouth he said through his clenched jaws, "Go ahead, put me in the fire. Fire is my friend. It just makes me stronger."

"Oh," said the man, "then I am not going to put you in the fire. But what can I do to kill you?"

"Oh," said Turtle, "whatever you do, do not put me in the water. I am afraid of the water. Oh, I am so afraid of the water!"

"Aha!" said the man. "I am smarter than you. I will take you down and drown you in the river."

"No," cried Turtle. "No!"

Still Turtle did not let go, and the man dragged him, kicking and scratching, all the way down to the river.

He waded in until Turtle was deep under the surface. When he was deep enough, Turtle let go and swam away. Ever since then, if you walk down by the river, you might see Turtle there, sitting on a log or sitting on a rock. You may notice he still has his cheeks painted red as if he wants to go to war. But if he sees you, he will

leap into the water and swim away underneath its surface as fast as he can, to show that Turtle has no desire anymore to make war on human beings. And another thing is true: You will no longer see Turtle paddling a canoe.

That is how that story of Turtle's war party goes. *Ho? Hey*.

CHIPMUNK AND BEAR

Long ago, back in the days when the animals could talk, Bear was out walking around. As he walked, Bear was boasting. "Hmmph!" he said. "I am the strongest of all the animals. Hmmph!" he said. "I am the biggest of all the animals. Hmmph!" he said. "I can do anything because I am Bear. If I want anyone to do my bidding, I only have to tell them because I am Bear. I, Bear, can do anything."

Just as Bear said that, a little voice down near the ground spoke up. It said, "You cannot do everything." Bear looked down. There was Chipmunk, sticking his head out of his hole.

Bear looked down at him and said, "I, Bear, can do anything I wish."

"If this is so," said Chipmunk, "can you tell the sun not to come up in the morning?"

Bear thought for a moment and said, "Yes. That I can do. I, Bear, can tell the sun not to rise. In fact, tomorrow, the sun will not come up."

"That is good," said Chipmunk. "I will stay and watch." And the two sat down right there. The sun was just going down, and Bear and Chipmunk turned to face the east and wait for the sun not to come up the next morning.

As they sat there through the night, Bear was chanting under his breath. He was saying, "The sun will not come up. The sun will not come up. I, Bear, command it. The sun will not come up."

But sitting next to him, Chipmunk was chanting under his breath, "The sun is going to rise. The sun is going to rise. Bear will be foolish. The sun is going to rise."

And as the night ended, a little bit of light began to appear there

in the east. Bear began to chant louder, "The sun will not come up. The sun will not come up." But little Chipmunk next to him was saying, "The sun is going to rise. The sun is going to rise."

As Bear chanted as hard as he could, facing the direction of the sun and telling it not to come up, the sun lifted above the horizon. It was a new day, and the sun had come up.

Chipmunk began to laugh. He rolled over and over with laughter. "Bear is a fool!" he said. "Bear is so foolish! The sun came up, the sun came up! The sun came up!"

Suddenly *Whomp!* a big paw came down on top of Chipmunk. Bear looked down as he held Chipmunk there on the ground, and he said, "Indeed the sun did come up. But you will never see another sunrise!"

Chipmunk knew now how foolish he had been. He thought quickly. "Oh Bear," he said, "you are right to kill me. I am a foolish little Chipmunk. I am worthless and I mean nothing in the world. You, Bear, are the greatest of all, and if only you would lift your paw a little bit so that I could catch my breath, I would tell you how

wonderful you are before you kill me."

Bear said, "That is a good idea." He lifted up his paw just a little bit, and Chipmunk scooted out and ran for his hole as fast as he could go. Bear's big paw whipped out and *Whoosh!* Bear's claws scraped right down Chipmunk's back just as he dove into his hole.

Chipmunk stayed in his hole all through the winter while those wounds on his back healed up. And when he came out in the spring, he had stripes on his back. To this day, if you see Chipmunk, you will see those stripes, and it may remind you, as it reminds Chipmunk, to be careful whom you make fun of. You may be the one who is foolish in the long run.

That is how that story of Chipmunk and Bear goes. *Ho? Hey.*

RABBIT'S SNOW DANCE

Back in the old days, Rabbit did not look as he does today. In the old days, Rabbit had long legs and a long bushy tail. And he was the fastest runner of all the animals. But in one way Rabbit was as he is today. Of all the things Rabbit loved to do, he loved to run around in the fresh new snow.

Now, if you have a field near your house and the snow has fallen, look out there in the morning. You'll see Rabbit's tracks all across that new snow, because rabbits love to run around and play when the snow falls.

One day, long ago, Rabbit was out walking around. It was near the end of winter, and all the snow had melted away. And as Rabbit

walked, he said to himself, "If only it would snow, then I could run around and play. If only it would snow."

Then, Rabbit remembered something. His grandmother had told him, "Rabbit, if you sing a little song in the right way, if you dance a little dance in the right way, sometimes you can make things happen." Rabbit said to himself, "I wonder if I could make it snow."

So Rabbit made up a song right then and there. He began to dance in a circle, and as he did so he sang this song:

> *"If only it would snow*
> *If only it would snow*
> *Then I could run around and play*
> *If only it would snow."*

As he sang and as he danced, he looked up, and he saw that some clouds were beginning to form in the sky. So he sang and danced a little harder:

> *"If only it would snow*
> *If only it would snow*

Then I could run around and play
If only it would snow."

Now a few flakes began to fall out of the sky. Rabbit was very happy—he sang and danced even harder!

"If only it would snow
If only it would snow
Then I could run around and play
If only it would snow.

"If only it would snow
If only it would snow
Then I could run around and play
If only it would snow."

Now the snow was falling hard. Flakes the size of feathers were floating down, covering the ground. But Rabbit was not satisfied. He wanted more. He sang his song again:

"If only it would snow
If only it would snow

Then I could run around and play
If only it would snow."

The snow fell. It fell harder and harder. It covered the ground completely, but Rabbit continued to dance and sing. It covered up the bushes, but Rabbit continued to dance and sing. It covered up the lower branches of the trees, but Rabbit still sang and danced. It snowed and snowed and snowed until it had covered all the trees in the forest. All that could be seen was just one little branch of a single tree, sticking up above the snow. And Rabbit, who had sung and danced his way to the top of all the snow, looked around and was very pleased. "Hmmph," Rabbit said, "I have done well."

But now Rabbit was tired. He wanted to take a nap. And where was his home? Way down below all that snow! He looked around, and, seeing the branch of that tree, he climbed up on top of it, curled himself up, and went to sleep.

While he slept, the sun came out. It shone down onto the Earth. It shone down onto all that new snow. Warmer and warmer the sun shone, and the snow began to melt away. It melted down below the

tops of the trees. It melted down below the branches of the trees. It melted down below the bushes. It melted down to the ground, and then it all melted away. And that was when Rabbit woke up.

Rabbit looked around and saw he was in the top of a tree! Even back then when Rabbit had long legs and a big bushy tail, Rabbit did not know how to climb trees, either up them or down them. "How can I get out of the top of this tree?" he wondered.

Now, he thought about singing his song and dancing his dance again but there was no room in the top of the tree to do that dance. He thought, "Maybe I can jump down." He looked way down, and there near the base of the tree he saw some new green plants. The sun had made them grow. They were just the kind of plant that Rabbit loved to eat.

"Ohh," he thought, and he remembered how hungry he was. "Maybe I *could* jump down," he said. He began to lean over, getting ready to try to jump, but as he leaned, his foot slipped, and his tail caught in the branches, and *Pop!* his tail broke right off. Rabbit fell down so hard that when he hit the ground, it pushed his front legs

in, it scrunched his back legs up, and he hit his nose so hard he split his lip.

Now, ever since then, that's how Rabbit has looked. His legs pushed in, his nose split, and his tail just a little stub, no longer long as it was before. But if you look up in the tops of certain trees at that time of year when the snow is just getting ready to melt, you will see little rabbit tails still hanging there to remind you to be satisfied with enough of a good thing. The little rabbit-tail trees—some people call them pussy willows—are there in 'the forest to remind you of this story.

And that's how that story goes. *Ho? Hey.*